LOUIE & DAN
Are FRIENDS

by Bonnie Pryor ❧ illustrated by Elizabeth Miles

MORROW JUNIOR BOOKS
NEW YORK

Watercolor pencil on Arches 90 lb hot press paper were used for the full-color illustrations.
The text type is 16-point Goudy Old Style.

Printed in Singapore at Tien Wah Press.

1 3 5 7 9 10 8 6 4 2

Library of Congress Cataloging-in-Publication Data
Pryor, Bonnie.
Louie & Dan are friends / by Bonnie Pryor; illustrated by Elizabeth Miles.
p. cm.
Summary: Most of the time two brothers live happily together even
though Dan loves to go exploring and Louie is a stay-at-home mouse.
ISBN 0-688-08560-1 (trade)—ISBN 0-688-08561-X (library)
[1. Brothers—Fiction.   2. Friendship—Fiction.   3. Mice—Fiction.
4. Family life—Fiction.]   I. Miles, Elizabeth J., ill.   II. Title.
PZ7.P94965Lq 1997   [E]—dc20   96-32444   CIP AC

To Debbie G., my right-hand woman

—B.P.

For Marla

—E.M.

Not so very long ago Louie and Dan left their mama's house and moved to a lovely new house under the roots of an old maple tree. Most of the time the two brothers were happy living together in their cozy home, even though Dan loved to go exploring and Louie was a stay-at-home sort of mouse.

One day Louie was sweeping the floor. As he swept, he sang a little song.

> "I'm a happy little mouse
> cleaning my pretty house.
> With my broom I sweep the floor
> and whisk the dirt right out the door."

"Mama Mouse used to sing that song," said Dan.
Thinking about Mama Mouse made Louie and Dan homesick.
Louie put away his broom and made them some tea. "I miss Mama Mouse," he said. "I even miss all our noisy brothers and sisters."

"Me too," Dan said. "Do you remember when Baby Mouse swung from the chandelier?"

"Yes," said Louie. "Do you remember how Mama Mouse always told us to be careful of cats and owls?"

Dan saw a tear in Louie's eye. "We could invite Mama Mouse for a visit."

"I'll write a letter right now!" Louie said. And he did.

They mailed the letter together.

The next morning Louie got up early. He looked around their house with a frown. This house is a mess! he thought. When Mama Mouse comes for a visit, the whole place should be sparkling clean.

Dan had also gotten up early. He saw Louie's frown. Maybe Louie is still homesick, Dan thought. I was planning to go exploring today, but Louie is my brother and my best friend. I'll stay home today and help him clean.

All morning Dan stayed home with Louie. He made their breakfast, but he forgot the dirty dishes and left them all for Louie to wash. When Louie dusted a chair, Dan was in the way. Dan swept the floor, but he left so many crumbs that Louie had to do it all over again. Worst of all, Dan talked so much that Louie couldn't think of a single song.

All this made Louie feel very grouchy. I wish Dan would go exploring, he thought.

Dan looked at his brother. He'd tried his best, but Louie still didn't
look happy. Just then there was a knock on the door. "I am your new
neighbor," said Mrs. Shrew. She was wearing her best hat and gloves.
She gave Louie a big plate of cookies. "I made them for you myself,"
she said. "Would you like the recipe?"

Louie made them all some tea. Mrs. Shrew gave Louie her favorite recipes. She had brought some old pinecones, and she showed Louie how to make a centerpiece for the table with them.

"Oh, dear," said Mrs. Shrew. "I see a cobweb in that corner."

"I haven't been able to reach it," Louie answered. He was so embarrassed his ears turned pink.

Mrs. Shrew reached into her purse. She pulled out a big feather duster. "Keep it," she said. "I have plenty."

Mrs. Shrew stayed all day. She and Louie talked about brooms and dusting and polish. They talked about curtains and rugs and cooking. Mrs. Shrew gave Louie seventeen recipes for fixing bread crumbs and thirty-two recipes using nuts. Louie enjoyed the visit immensely, but Dan was so bored he didn't know what to do. He sat in a chair and tried not to fall asleep. Mrs. Shrew is a better friend than I am for Louie, he thought sadly.

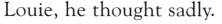

The next morning Louie got up early. Dan stayed home with me even though he is not a stay-at-home sort of mouse, Louie thought. So today I will go exploring with him.

After breakfast the two brothers put on their coats and went out to explore the neighborhood. They had not gone very far when Dan spied something shiny poking out of some rocks. He scratched at the dirt.

"Look, Louie. It's a beautiful gold button."

"Ohh." Louie shuddered. "Don't touch it. It's probably covered with *germs*."

Then Dan found a hollow log twisting under a pile of leaves. Dan peeked inside. It looked very interesting.

"Don't go in there," Louie cried. "It's too dark." He was trying to enjoy exploring with Dan, but everything looked scary and wild.

"My feet hurt," he said in a grumpy voice. "I think we should go home."

The next morning Louie was outside sweeping the porch when Chester Squirrel walked by. "I am your new neighbor," said Chester. "Would you like to go exploring with me?"

"Oh, no," Louie said quickly. "But my brother loves to explore."

Louie introduced Chester to Dan. "I have a great idea," Chester said. "I know a place in the man's garden that is full of tasty sunflower seeds. He puts them there for the birds."

"What is a man?" asked Dan. "I don't remember Mama Mouse telling us about a man."

"Don't worry," said Chester. "Men are big and scary, but they can't run very fast. If the man comes, we'll just run away."

At the edge of the forest, Chester stopped. He pointed to a tall pole with a little house on the top. "All we have to do is climb up that tree and drop down."

Chester zipped up the tree. He ran down a branch hanging over the little house. Then he made a giant leap and landed right in a big pile of seeds. "Come on," he said, stuffing his mouth. "They're delicious."

Dan looked at the tree. It was very high for a little mouse. Bravely he started to climb. He looked down and thought about all the places a little mouse could hide. Carefully he crept across the branch. He could see piles of lovely seeds. It made his mouth water just thinking about all that crunchy goodness. But it was much too far for a little mouse to jump.

Suddenly there was a shadow on the seed-house wall, and then two crows landed right on top. "*Caw,*" they screamed. "*Thief, thief.* Those are our seeds."

Chester stuffed another bite in his mouth. "Go away," he scolded. "I was here first."

The crows had mean black eyes and long sharp beaks. They were not bigger than Chester. But they were much bigger than Dan. They rose high into the air, then swooped down toward Dan's branch. "*Thief, thief,*" they screamed. As they came closer and closer, Dan shut his eyes. He wished he was safe in his little house. He wished Louie was there to help him.

Suddenly the crows flapped away. "*Man, man,*" they screeched. Dan opened his eyes wide. Walking straight toward the tree was the biggest creature he had ever seen. Worst of all, following right behind was a cat!

"Run for your life," shouted Chester.

Dan scrambled down the tree. His heart was pounding so hard he could hardly catch his breath. He ran all the way to his cozy house and slammed the door.

"Did you have fun exploring today?" Louie asked.

Dan did not want Louie to know how frightened he'd been. "I had a wonderful time," he said. His knees were shaking so much he went straight to bed.

Chester is a better friend than I am for Dan, Louie thought sadly.

Early the next morning there was a knock at the door. "It's Mama Mouse," Louie shouted happily. All of their brothers and sisters came too. There was lots of hugging and laughing and hugging some more.

Mama Mouse stayed all day. The brothers and sisters played hide-and-seek in the kitchen. Some of them played cat-and-mouse in the living room and sang mouse songs on the porch. Baby Mouse jumped on the beds and scribbled with a crayon on the wall.

Louie and Dan told Mama Mouse about their new friends. "Chester likes to go exploring," Louie said. "He is a good friend for Dan."

"Mrs. Shrew likes cooking and cleaning, just like Louie," said Dan.

"I guess we can't really be best friends," said Louie.

Mama Mouse gave them both a hug. "Nonsense," she said to Louie. "When you are done being a stay-at-home sort of mouse and Dan is done exploring, what do you both like to do best?"

"I like it when Dan tells me about his adventures," said Louie.

"I like it when Louie makes us a cup of tea and sings his songs," said Dan.

Mama Mouse smiled. "It's always nice to share the day with your best friend."

By the time Mama Mouse and all the sisters and brothers went home, Louie and Dan were worn-out.

Louie washed the cups and put them away. He sang a little song while he worked.

> "My house is nice and quiet.
> I like it just that way.
> It's nice to have some company
> and nice to see them go away."

"That sounds like a happy song," said Dan.

"Of course," said Louie. "All my songs are happy songs."

Louie and Dan climbed in their beds. "I made up a happy song too," Dan said shyly. He sang it for Louie.

"Sometimes we're together.
Sometimes we're apart.
But we know we are best friends
down deep in our heart."

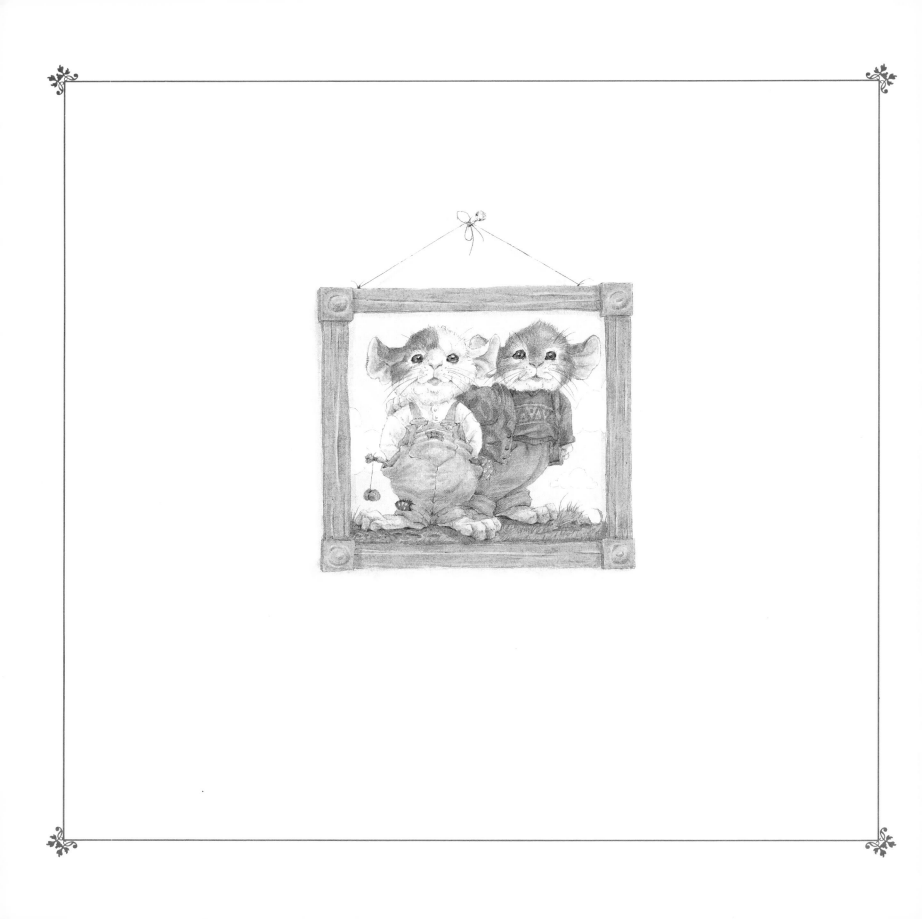